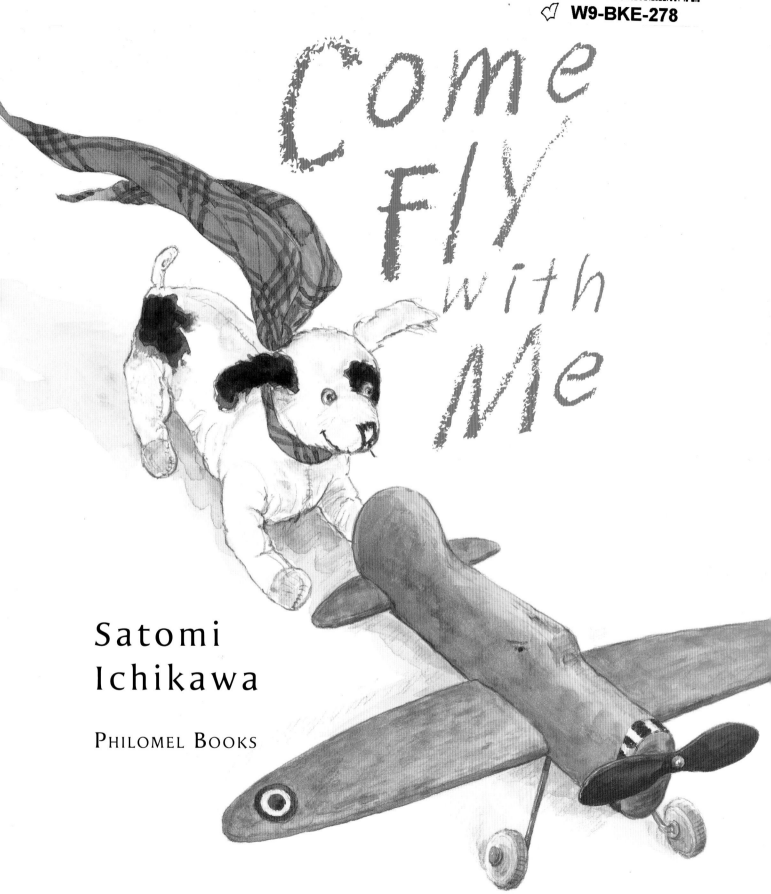

Come Fly with Me

Satomi
Ichikawa

PHILOMEL BOOKS

"I have had enough," says Cosmos, the wooden plane, jumping from the toy box.

Woggy, the stuffed dog and his best friend, jumps out after him. "What's the matter?" Woggy asks.

"I have never left this playroom—I want to go Somewhere."

From the balcony Woggy looks at the White Dome on the hilltop. "That's Somewhere!" he says.

There is a growling noise over them.

"I know what that's from," says Woggy. "An airplane! That plane is going Somewhere."

"An airplane! But *I'm* an airplane!" Cosmos says.

"So you are," says Woggy. "And you can go Somewhere, too."

"You're my best friend. I'll help you," says Woggy.
"Come fly with me, too," says Cosmos.

Woggy winds the propeller and pushes Cosmos to the edge of the balcony. "Are you ready?"

"Yes," says Cosmos. And off the two friends go.

"I can fly! I can fly!" sings Cosmos happily.

"What Somewhere are you going to?" shouts Woggy.

"To the White Dome, of course!"

"Higher than these stairs . . ."

"and higher than these windows . . ."

"Even higher than these rooftops!"
"Two friends on their way,"
shouts Cosmos. "Nothing can stop us now!"

"But look, Woggy, birds!" says Cosmos. "I can do that, too!"

"Oh, oh," says Woggy. "Whoaaaaa."

Then they hear a growling noise behind them.

"Another plane?" roars Cosmos. "I'll outrace him."

"Oh, dear," says Woggy. "It doesn't sound like a plane.
And it's coming after us!"

"It's a cloud monster," says Woggy. "It's going to capture us!"

"Not as long as we have each other," says Cosmos. "Hang on!"

The cloud monster blows them topsy and turvy and around and around and around.

"Together through thick and thin," shouts Woggy.
"Through thin and thick," sputters Cosmos.

Until *down, DOWN, and DOWN*

the two friends go.

"We'll never get Somewhere now," sobs Cosmos.
"True," says Woggy.

"But look. Sunshine! And the Dome!"
Woggy rewinds Cosmos, pushes him to the edge of the
roof, and jumps on.

"Finally," the two friends shout. "Somewhere!"

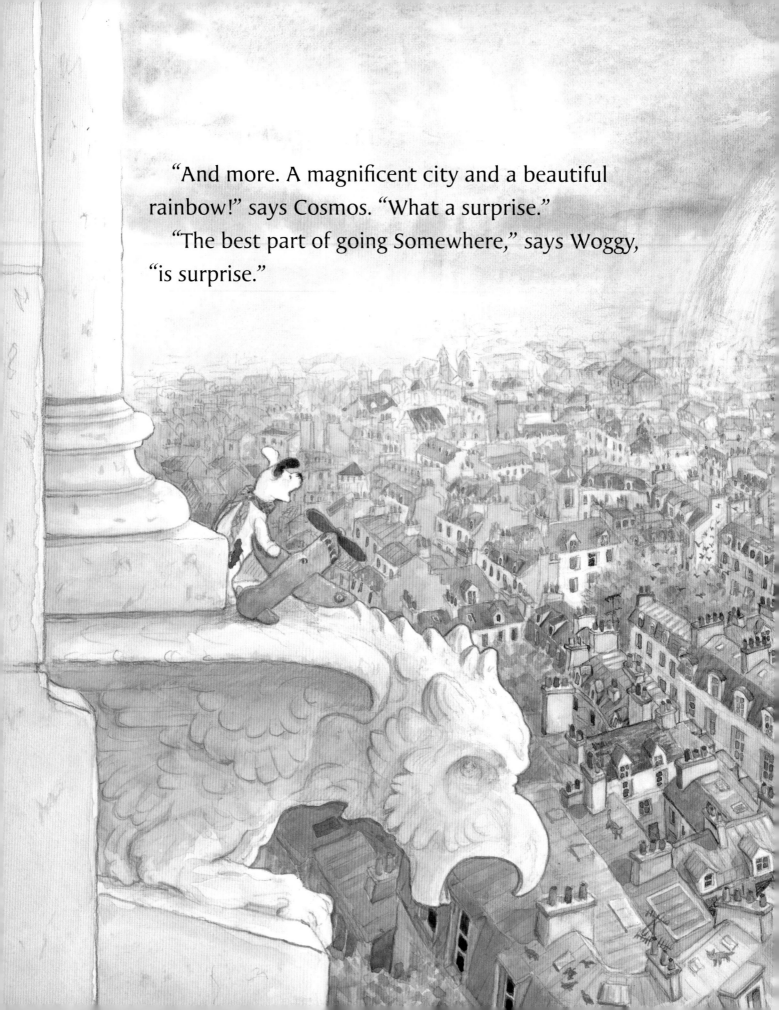

"And more. A magnificent city and a beautiful rainbow!" says Cosmos. "What a surprise."

"The best part of going Somewhere," says Woggy, "is surprise."

"No, no," says Cosmos. "The best part of going
Somewhere is sharing it with friends."
"Right," says Woggy as they fly toward home.

Patricia Lee Gauch, editor

PHILOMEL BOOKS

A division of Penguin Young Readers Group.
Published by The Penguin Group.
Penguin Group (USA) Inc., 375 Hudson Street, New York, NY 10014, U.S.A.
Penguin Group (Canada), 90 Eglinton Avenue East, Suite 700, Toronto, Ontario M4P 2Y3, Canada (a division of Pearson Penguin Canada Inc.).
Penguin Books Ltd, 80 Strand, London WC2R 0RL, England.
Penguin Ireland, 25 St. Stephen's Green, Dublin 2, Ireland (a division of Penguin Books Ltd).
Penguin Group (Australia), 250 Camberwell Road, Camberwell, Victoria 3124, Australia (a division of Pearson Australia Group Pty Ltd).
Penguin Books India Pvt Ltd, 11 Community Centre, Panchsheel Park, New Delhi - 110 017, India.
Penguin Group (NZ), 67 Apollo Drive, Rosedale, North Shore 0745, Auckland, New Zealand (a division of Pearson New Zealand Ltd.)
Penguin Books (South Africa) (Pty) Ltd, 24 Sturdee Avenue, Rosebank, Johannesburg 2196, South Africa.
Penguin Books Ltd, Registered Offices: 80 Strand, London WC2R 0RL, England.

Manufactured in China by South China Printing Co. Ltd. Design by Semadar Megged.
The illustrations are rendered in watercolor.   Library of Congress Cataloging-in-Publication Data

ISBN 978-0-399-24679-1
3 5 7 9 10 8 6 4 2

To my dear readers,

From my window, I see the white dome on the hilltop. It stands there always, no matter whether it is sunny, cloudy, windy, misty, rainy, stormy, or snowy.

I live in an apartment behind the dome with my little friends. Some might say they are just stuffed animals, toys, and dolls, but for me, they have come through many difficult moments, lonely days, and even happy events. After long years together, I call them friends. I love them. They know everything about me, and I can guess what they think, even if they can't say a word.

As I sit at my drawing table, I look at the white dome through my window and sometimes sigh, "If I could only go somewhere like those birds . . ."

Among my little friends are the wooden plane and the stuffed dog that shake their heads and wings at me, telling me, "Yes! Yes! Yes! We want to go somewhere like those birds!" So in this book I finally let them go flying. But me, I have to stay here and keep working . . . so we can find out how their adventure goes.

Montmartre in Paris